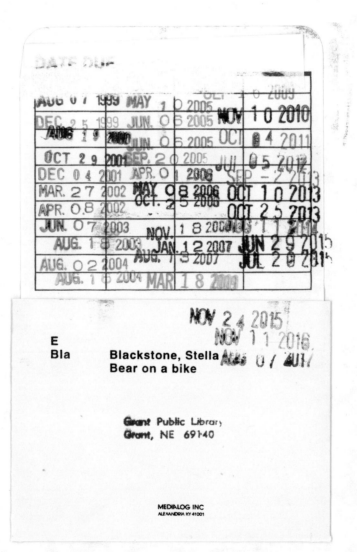

# BEAR ON A BIKE

## Written by Stella Blackstone
## Illustrated by Debbie Harter

**BAREFOOT BOOKS**

Bear on a bike,
As happy as can be,
Where are you going, bear?
Please wait for me!

I'm going to the market,
Where fruit and flowers are sold,
Where people buy fresh oranges
And pots of marigold.

Bear on a raft,
As happy as can be,
Where are you going, bear?
Please wait for me!

I'm going to the forest,
Where fearsome creatures prowl,
Where racoons play and bobcats snarl
And hungry foxes howl.

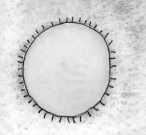

Bear on a wagon,
As happy as can be,
Where are you going, bear?
Please wait for me!

I'm going to the prairie,
Where wild buffaloes roam,
Where graceful eagles soar and glide
And prairie dogs make their home.

Bear in a steam train,
As happy as can be,
Where are you going, bear?
Please wait for me!

I'm going to the seaside,
Where children love to play,
Where young friends dig and race
And swim, while fishes dart away.

Bear on a boat,
As happy as can be,
Where are you going, bear?
Please wait for me!

I'm going to an island,
Where magic star fruits grow,
Where herons fish in secret groves
And sparkling rivers flow.

Bear in a balloon,
As happy as can be,
Where are you going, bear?
Please wait for me!

I'm going to a rainbow,
Where the earth meets the sky,
Where the clouds turn into rain
And bright-winged parrots fly.

Bear in a carriage,
As happy as can be,
Where are you going, bear?
Please wait for me!

I'm going to a castle,
Where night is turned to day,
Where princes and princesses dance
And merry music plays.

Bear on a rocket,
Flying through the night,
Wherever you are going, bear,
Goodbye and goodnight!

Barefoot Beginners
an imprint of
Barefoot Books Inc.
41, Schermerhorn Street, Suite 145
Brooklyn, New York
NY 11201-4845

Graphic design by Jennie Hoare
Color reproduction by Unifoto, Cape Town
Printed and bound in Singapore by Tien Wah Press

ISBN 1 901223 49 3

1 3 5 7 9 8 6 4 2

17930